Caroline S. Norton

The Lady of La Garaye

Caroline S. Norton

The Lady of La Garaye

ISBN/EAN: 9783337284657

Printed in Europe, USA, Canada, Australia, Japan

Cover: Foto ©Andreas Hilbeck / pixelio.de

More available books at **www.hansebooks.com**

THE

LADY OF LA GARAYE.

BY

THE HON MRS. NORTON.

NEW YORK:

ANSON D. F. RANDOLPH AND CO.

PRESSWORK BY JOHN WILSON AND SON,
UNIVERSITY PRESS.

TO

THE MOST NOBLE

THE MARQUIS OF LANSDOWNE,

𝕿𝖍𝖎𝖘 𝕷𝖎𝖙𝖙𝖑𝖊 𝕻𝖔𝖊𝖒

IS AFFECTIONATELY AND GRATEFULLY

INSCRIBED.

DEDICATION.

Friend of old days, of suffering, storm, and strife,
   Patient and kind through many a wild appeal;
In the arena of thy brilliant life
   Never too busy or too cold to feel:

Companion from whose ever-teeming store
   Of thought and knowledge, happy memory brings
So much of social wit and sage's lore,
   Garnered and gleaned by me as precious things:

Kinsman of him whose very name soon grew
   Unreal as music heard in pleasant dreams,
So vain the hope my girlish fancy drew,
   So faint and far his vanished presence seems:

To thee I dedicate this record brief
   Of foreign scenes and deeds too little known;

This tale of noble souls who conquered grief
  By dint of tending sufferings not their own.

Thou hast known all my life: its pleasant hours,
  (How many of them have I owed to thee!)
Its exercise of intellectual powers,
  With thoughts of fame and gladness not to be.

Thou knowest how Death forever dogged my way,
  And how of those I loved the best, and those
Who loved and pitied *me* in life's young day,
  Narrow, and narrower still, the circle grows.

Thou knowest—for thou hast proved—the dreary
      shade
  A first-born's loss casts over lonely days;
And gone is now the pale fond smile, that made
  In my dim future, yet, a path of rays.

Gone, the dear comfort of a voice whose sound
  Came like a beacon-bell, heard clear above
The whirl of violent waters surging round;
  Speaking to shipwrecked ears of help and love.

The joy that budded on my own youth's bloom,
　　When life wore still a glory and a gloss,
Is hidden from me in the silent tomb;
　　Smiting with premature unnatural loss,

So that my very soul is wrung with pain,
　　Meeting old friends whom most I love to see.
Where are the younger lives, since these remain?
　　I weep the eyes that should have wept for me!

But all the more I cling to those who speak,
　　Like thee, in tones unaltered by my change;
Greeting my saddened glance, and faded cheek,
　　With the same welcome that seemed sweet and
　　　　strange

In early days: when I, of gifts made proud,
　　That could the notice of such men beguile,
Stood listening to thee in some brilliant crowd,
　　With the warm triumph of a youthful smile.

Oh! little now remains of all that was!
　　Even for this gift of linking measured words,

My heart oft questions, with discouraged pause,
   Does music linger in the slackening chords?

Yet, friend, I feel not that all power is fled,
   While offering to thee, for the kindly years,
The intangible gift of thought, whose silver thread
   Heaven keeps untarnished by our bitterest tears.

So, in the brooding calm that follows woe,
   This tale of LA GARAYE I fain would tell,—
As, when some earthly storm hath ceased to blow,
   And the huge mounting sea hath ceased to swell;

After the maddening wrecking and the roar,
   The wild high dash, the moaning sad retreat,
Some cold slow wave creeps faintly to the shore,
   And leaves a white shell at the gazer's feet.

Take, then, the poor gift in thy faithful hand;
   Measure its worth not merely by my own,
But hold it dear as gathered from the sand
   Where so much wreck of youth and hope lies
      strown.

So, if in years to come my words abide—
   Words of the dead to stir some living brain—
When thoughtful readers lay my book aside,
   Musing on all it tells of joy and pain,

Towards thee, good heart, towards thee their
         thoughts shall roam,
   Whose unforsaking faith time hath not riven ;
And to their minds this just award shall come,
   'Twas a TRUE friend to whom such thanks were
         given!

INTRODUCTION.

IT is pleasant to me to be able to assure my readers that the story I have undertaken to versify is in no respect a fiction. I have added nothing to the beautiful and striking simplicity of the events it details. I have respected that mournful "romance of real life" too much to spoil its lessons by any poetical licence. Nothing is mine in this story but the language in which it is told. The portrait of the Countess de la Garaye is copied from an authentic picture preserved in one of the religious houses of Dinan, in Brittany, where the Hospital of Incurables, founded by her and her husband, still subsists. The ruined château and its ivy-covered gateway are faithfully given, without embellishment or alteration, as they appeared when I saw them in the year 1860. The château is rapidly crumbling. The memory of the De la Garayes is fresh in the memory of the people.

They died within two years of each other, and
were buried among their poor in the district of
Taden; having, both during their lives and by will
after death, contributed the greater part of their
fortune to the wisest and most carefully conducted
charities. Among the bequests left by the Count
de la Garaye, was one especially interesting to this
country; for he left a large sum to the prisoners of
Rennes and Dinan, consisting principally of English
officers and soldiers, who were suffering in these
crowded foreign jails all the horrors which the
philanthropic Howard endeavored to reform in his
own land; and which at one time caused a sort of
plague to break out in Dinan. This humane be-
quest is the more remarkable, as the Count was, in
spite of the gentleness and generosity of his feelings towards imprisoned foes, patriotic enough to
insist on marching to oppose the landing of the
English on the coast of France in 1746, though he
was then upwards of seventy years of age!

He was of noble family, being the younger son
of Guillaume Marot, Count de la Garaye, Governor
of the town and castle of Dinan;—that strong
fortress which Anne of Brittany, in her threatened

dominions, playfully termed the "key of her casket." By the death of his elder brother, he became inheritor of the family honors, and married Mademoiselle de la Motte-Piquet, niece of the Chevalier de la Motte-Piquet, who so greatly distinguished himself in the American war. Claude-Toussaint, Count de la Garaye, was a man personally attractive in appearance and manner, and very dexterous in fencing and feats of horsemanship. To the plaintive beauty of his wife's portrait I have scarcely been able to render justice, even with the advantage of its being engraved by Mr. Shaw.

Those who may desire to read the narrative in plain prose, will find a notice of the Château de la Garaye in the "Recherches sur Dinan et ses Environs," by Luigi Odorici, Curator of the Museum of that town, and in the travelling guide lately issued by M. Peignet, both works published on the spot. Allusion is also made to the story, or rather to the beneficent works of charity performed by the De la Garayes, in Madame de Genlis' "Adèle et Theodore;" but inasmuch as she has totally altered the real circumstances, and attributed these holy deeds to the result of grief for the loss of a daughter, even while admitting in a foot-note that she is aware the De la Garayes never had a child, and that all is her own invention, I do not think it necessary further to allude to her version of the tale; more striking in its unadorned truth than all the art of the poet or romancist could make it.

The Lady of La Garaye.

UINS! A charm is in the word:
It makes us smile, it makes us sigh;
'Tis like the note of some spring
bird

Recalling other Springs gone by.
And other wood-notes which we heard
With some sweet face in some green lane,
And never can so hear again!

Ruins! They were not desolate
To us,—the ruins we remember:
Early we came and lingered late,
Through bright July, or rich September;
With young companions wild with glee,
We feasted 'neath some spreading tree—

And looked into their laughing eyes,
And mocked the echo for replies.
Oh! eyes—and smiles—and days of yore,
Can nothing your delight restore?
Return!

      Return? In vain we listen;
Those voices have been lost to earth!
Our hearts may throb—our eyes may glisten,
They'll call no more in love or mirth.
For, like a child sent out to play,
Our youth hath had its holiday,
And silence deepens where we stand
Lone as in some foreign land,
Where our language is not spoken,
And none know our hearts are broken.

Ruins! How we loved them then!
How we loved the haunted glen
Which gray towers overlook,
Mirrored in the glassy brook!
How we dreamed,—and how we guessed,
Looking up, with earnest glances,
Where the black crow built its nest,

And we built our wild romances;
Tracing in the crumbled dwelling
Bygone tales of no one's telling!

This was the Chapel: that the stair.
Here, where all lies damp and bare,
The fragrant thurible was swung,
The silver lamp in beauty hung,
And in that mass of ivied shade
The pale nuns sang—the abbot prayed.

This was the Kitchen.   Cold and blank
The huge hearth yawns; and wide and high,
The chimney shows the open sky;
There daylight peeps through many a crank
Where birds immund find shelter dank,
And when the moonlight shineth through,
Echoes the wild tu-whit to-whoo
Of mournful owls, whose languid flight
Scarce stirs the silence of the night.

This is the Courtyard,—damp and drear!
The men-at-arms were mustered here;

2

Here would the fretted war-horse bound,
Starting to hear the trumpet sound;
And captains, then of warlike fame,
Clanked and glittered as they came.
Forgotten names! forgotten wars!
Forgotten gallantry and scars!
How is your little busy day
Perished and crushed and swept away!

Here is the Lady's Chamber, whence
With looks of lovely innocence
Some heroine our fancy dresses
In golden locks or raven tresses,
And pearl embroidered silks and stuffs,
And quaintly quilted sleeves and ruffs,
Looked forth to see retainers go,
Or trembled at the assaulting foe.

This was the Dungeon; deep and dark!
Where the starved prisoner moaned in vain
Until Death left him stiff and stark,
Unconscious of the galling chain
By which the thin, bleached bones were bound
When chance revealed them under ground.

Oh! Time, oh! ever-conquering Time!
These men had once their prime:
But now, succeeding generations hear
Beneath the shadow of each crumbling arch
The music low and drear,
The muffled music of thy onward march,
Made up of piping winds and rustling leaves
And plashing rain-drops falling from slant eaves,
And all mysterious unconnected sounds
With which the place abounds.
Time doth efface
Each day some lingering trace
Of human government and human care:
The things of air
And earth, usurp the walls to be their own;
Creatures that dwell alone,
Occupy boldly: every mouldering nook
Wherein we peer and look,
Seems with wild denizens so swarming rife,
We know the healthy stir of human life
Must be forever gone!
The walls where hung the warriors shining casques
Are green with moss and mould;

The blindworm coils where Queens have slept, nor
     asks
For shelter from the cold.
The swallow,—he is master all the day,
And the great owl is ruler through the night;
The little bat wheels on his circling way
With restless flittering flight;
And that small black bat, and the creeping things,
At will they come and go,
And the soft, white owl with velvet wings
And a shriek of human woe!
The brambles let no footstep pass
By that rent in the broken stair,
Where the pale tufts of the windle-strae grass
Hang like locks of dry dead hair;
But there the keen wind ever weeps and moans,
Working a passage through the mouldering stones.

Oh! Time, oh! conquering Time!
I know that wild wind's chime
Which, like a passing-bell,
Or distant knell,
Speaks to man's heart of Death and of Decay:

While thy step passes o'er the necks of Kings
And over common things,—
And into Earth's green orchards making way,
Halts, where the fruits of human hope abound,
And shakes their trembling ripeness to the ground

But hark—a sudden shout
Of laughter! and a nimble giddy rout,
Who know not yet what saddened hours may mean,
Come dancing through the scene!

Ruins! Ruins! let us roam
Through what was a human home.
What care we
How deep its depths of darkness be?
Follow! Follow!
Down the hollow
Through the bramble-fencing thorns
Where the white snail hides her horns;
Leap across the dreadful gap
To that corner's mossy lap,—
Do, and dare!
Clamber up the crumbling stair;

Trip along the narrow wall,
Where the sudden rattling fall
Of loosened stones, on winter nights,
In his dreams the peasant frights:
And push them, till their rolling sound,
Dull and heavy, beat the ground.

Now a song, high up and clear,
Like a lark's enchants the ear;
Or some happy face looks down,
Looking, oh! so fresh and fair,
Wearing youth's most glorious crown,
One rich braid of golden hair:
Or two hearts that wildly beat,
And two pair of eager feet,
Linger in the turret's bend
As they side by side ascend,
For the momentary bliss
Of a lover's stolen kiss;
And emerge into the shining
Of that summer day's declining,
Disengaging clasping hands
As they meet their comrade bands;

With the smile that lately hovered,
(Making lips and eyes so bright,)
And the blush which darkness covered
Mantling still in rosy light!

Ruins!   Oh! ye have your charm;
Death is cold, but life is warm;
And the fervent days we knew
Ere our hopes grew faint and few,
Claim even now a happy sigh,
Thinking of those hours gone by:
Of the wooing long since passed,—
Of the love that still shall last,—
Of the wooing and the winning,
Brightest end to bright beginning;
When the feet we sought to guide
Tripped so lightly by our side.
That, as swift they made their way
Through the path and tangled brake,
Safely we could swear and say
We loved all ruins for their sake!
Gentle hearts, one ruin more
From amongst so many score—

One, from out a host of names,
To your notice puts forth claims.
Come! with me make holiday,
In the woods of La Garaye,
Sit within those tangled bowers,
Where fleet by the silent hours,
Only broken by a song
From the chirping woodland throng.
Listen to the tale I tell:
Grave the story is—not sad ;
And the peasant plodding by
Greets the place with kindly eye
For the inmates that it had!

The Lady of La Garaye.

PART I.

N Dinan's walls the morning sunlight
    plays,
Gilds the stern fortress with a crown
    of rays,
Shines on the children's heads that
    troop to school,
Turns into beryl-brown the forest pool,
Sends diamond sparkles over gushing springs,
And showers down glory on the simplest things.
And many a young seigneur and damsel bold
See with delight those beams of reddening gold,
For they are bid to join the hunt to-day
By Claud Marot, the lord of La Garaye;
And merry is it in his spacious halls;

Cheerful the host, whatever sport befalls,

Cheerful and courteous, full of manly grace,

His heart's frank welcome written in his face;

So eager, that his pleasure never cloys,

But glad to share whatever he enjoys;

Rich, liberal, gayly dressed, of noble mien,

Clear eyes,—full curving mouth,—and brow serene;

Master of speech in many a foreign tongue,

And famed for feats of arms, although so young;

Dexterous in fencing. skilled in horsemanship—

His voice and hand preferred to spur or whip;

Quick at a jest and smiling repartee,

With a sweet laugh that sounded frank and free,

But holding Satire an accursed thing,

A poisoned javelin or a serpent's sting;

Pitiful to the poor; of courage high;

A soul that could all turns of fate defy:

Gentle to women: reverent to old age:

What more, young Claud, could men's esteem
        engage?

What more be given to bless thine earthly state,

Save Love, which still must crown the happiest fate!

Love, therefore, came. That sunbeam lit his life.

And where he wooed, he won, a gentle wife,
Born, like himself, of lineage brave and good
And like himself, of warm and eager mood;
Glad to share gladness, pleasure to impart,
With dancing spirits and a tender heart.
Pleased too to share the manlier sports which made
The joy of his young hours.   No more afraid
Of danger, than the seabird, used to soar
From the high rocks above the ocean's roar,
Which dips its slant wing in the wave's white crest,
And deems the foamy undulations, rest.

Nor think the feminine beauty of her soul
Tarnished by yielding to such joy's control;
Nor that the form which, like a flexile reed,
Swayed with the movements of her bounding steed
Took from those graceful hours a rougher force,
Or left her nature masculine and coarse.
She was not bold from boldness, but from love;
Bold from gay frolic; glad with him to rove
In danger or in safety, weal or woe,
And where he ventured, still she yearned to go.
Bold with the courage of his bolder life,

At home a tender and submissive wife;
Abroad, a woman, modest,—aye, and proud;
Not seeking homage from the casual crowd.
She remained pure, that darling of his sight,
In spite of boyish feats, and rash delight;
Still the eyes fell before an insolent look,
Or flashed their bright and innocent rebuke;
Still the cheek kept its delicate youthful bloom,
And the blush reddened through the snow-white
      plume.

He that had seen her, with her courage high,
First in the chase where all dashed rapid by,
He that had watched her bright impetuous look
When she prepared to leap the silver brook,—
Fair in her Spring-time as a branch of May;
Had felt the dull sneer feebly die away,
And unused kindly smiles upon his cold lips play.

God made all pleasures innocent; but man
Turns them to shame, since first our earth began
To shudder 'neath the stroke of delving tools,
When Eve and Adam lost—poor tempted fools—

The sweet safe shelter of their Eden bowers,
Its easy wealth of sun-ripe fruits and flowers,
For some forbidden zest that was not given,
Some riotous hope to make a mimic Heaven,
And sank,—from being wingless angels,—low
Into the depths of mean and abject woe.

Why should the sweet elastic sense of joy
Presage a fault? Why should the pleasure cloy,
Or turn to blame, which Heaven itself inspires,
Who gave us health and strength and all desires?
The children play, and sin not;—let the young
Still carol songs, as others too have sung;
Still urge the fiery courser o'er the plain,
Proud of his glossy sides and flowing mane;
Still, when they meet in careless hours of mirth,
Laugh, as if Sorrow were unknown to earth;
Prattling sweet nothings, which, like buds of flowers,
May turn to earnest thoughts and vigilant hours.
What boys can suffer, and weak women dare,
Let Indian and Crimean wastes declare:
Perchance in that gay group of laughters stand
Guides and defenders for our native laud;—

Folly it is to see a wit in woe,
And hold youth sinful for the spirits' flow.
As through the meadow-lands clear rivers run,
Blue in the shadow—silver in the sun—
Till, rolling by some pestilential source,
Some factory work whose wheels with horrid force
Strike the pure waters with their dripping beams,
Send poison gushing to the crystal streams,
And leave the innocent things to whom God gave
A natural home in that translucent wave
Gasping strange death, and floating down to show
The evil working in the depths below,—
So man can poison pleasure at its source;
Clog the swift sparkle of its rapid course,
Mix muddy morbid thoughts in vicious strife,
Till to the surface floats the death of life;—
But not the less the stream itself was pure—
And not the less may blameless joy endure.

Careless,—but not impure,—the joyous days
Passed in a rapturous whirl; a giddy maze,
Where the young Count and lovely Countess drew
A new delight from every pleasure new.

They woke to gladness as the morning broke;
Their very voices kept, whene'er they spoke,
A ring of joy, a harmony of life,
That made you bless the husband and the wife.
And every day the careless festal throng,
And every night the dance and feast and song,
Shared with young boon companions, marked the
        time
As with a carillon's exulting chime;
Where those two entered, gloom passed out of sight,
Chased by the glow of their intense delight.

So, till the day when over Dinan's walls
The Autumn sunshine of my story falls;
And the guests bidden, gather for the chase,
And the smile brightens on the lovely face
That greets them in succession as they come
Into that high and hospitable home.

Like a sweet picture doth the Lady stand,
Still blushing as she bows; one tiny hand,
Hid by a pearl-embroidered gauntlet, holds
Her whip, and her long robe's exuberant folds.

The other hand is bare, and from her eyes
Shades now and then the sun, or softly lies,
With a caressing touch, upon the neck
Of the dear glossy steed she loves to deck
With saddle-housings worked in golden thread,
And golden bands upon his noble head.
White is the little hand whose taper fingers
Smooth his fine coat,—and still the lady lingers,
Leaning against his side; nor lifts her head,
But gently turns as gathering footsteps tread;
Reminding you of doves with shifting throats,
Brooding in sunshine by their sheltering cotes.
Under her plumèd hat her wealth of curls
Falls down in golden links among her pearls,
And the rich purple of her velvet vest
Slims the young waist. and rounds the graceful
       breast.

So, till the latest joins the happy Meet;
Then springs she gladly to her eager feet;
And, while the white hand from her courser's side
Slips like a snow-flake,—stands prepared to ride.
Then lightly vaulting to her seat, she seems

Queen of some fair possession seen in dreams;
Queen of herself, and of the world; sweet Queen!
Her crown the plume above her brow serene,
Her jewelled whip a sceptre, and her dress
The regal mantle worn by loveliness.

And well she wears such mantle: swift her horse,
But firm her seat throughout the rapid course;
No rash unsteadiness, no shifting pose
Disturbs that line of beauty as she goes:
She wears her robe as some fair sloop her sails,
Which swell and flutter to the rising gales,
But never from the cordage taut and trim
Slacken or swerve away.   The evening dim
Sees her return, unwearied and unbent,
The fair folds falling smooth as when she went;
The little foot no clasping buckle keeps,
She frees it, and to earth untrammelled leaps.

Alas! look well upon that picture fair!
The face—the form—the smile—the golden hair;
The agile beauty of each movement made,—
The loving softness of her eyes' sweet shade,

3

The bloom and pliant grace of youthful days,
The gladness and the glory of her gaze.
If we knew when the last time was the last,
Visions so dear to straining eyes went past;
If we knew when the horror and the gloom
Should overcast the pride of beauty's bloom;
If we knew when affection nursed in vain
Should grow to be but bitterness and pain;
It were a curse to blight all living hours
With a hot dust, like dark volcano showers.
Give thanks to God who blinded us with Hope:
Denied man skill to draw his horoscope;
And, to keep mortals of the present fond,
Forbid the keenest sight to pierce beyond!

Falsehood from those we trusted; cruel sneers
From those whose voice was music to our ears;
Lonely old age; oppressed and orphaned youth;
Yearning appeals to hearts that know no ruth;
Ruin, that starves pale mouths we loved to feed;
A friend's forsaking in our utmost need;
These come,—and sting,—and madden; aye, and
          slay;

But not the less our joy hath had its day;
No little cloud first flecked our tranquil skies,
Presaging shipwreck to the prophet eyes;
No hand came forth upon the walls of home
With vanishing radiance writing darkest doom;
No child-soul called us in the dead of night,
Thrilled with a message from a God of might;
No shrouded Seer, by some enforcing spell,
Rose from Death's rest, Life's restless chance to tell:
The lightning smote us—shivering stem and bough:
All was so green: all lies so blighted now!

They ride together all that sunny day,
Claud and the lovely Lady of Garaye;
O'er hill and dale,—through fields of late reaped
    corn,
Through woods—wherever sounds the hunting-horn.
Wherever scour the fleet hounds, fast they follow,
Through tufted thickets and the leaf-strewn hollow;
And thrice,—the game secured,—they rest awhile,
And slacken bridle with a breathless smile;
And thrice, with joyous speed, off, off they go,—
Like a fresh arrow from a new-strung bow!

But now the ground is rough with boulder stones,
Where, wild beneath, the prisoned streamlet moans,
The prisoned streamlet struggling to be free,
Baring the roots of many a toppling tree,
Breaking the line where smooth-barked saplings
  rank,
And undermining all the creviced bank;
Till gushing out at length to open space,
Mad with the effort of its desperate race,
It pauses, swelling o'er the narrow ridge
Where fallen branches make a natural bridge,
Leaps to the next descent, and balked no more,
Foams to a waterfall, whose ceaseless roar
Echoes far down the banks, and through the forest
  hoar!

Across the water full of peakèd stones—
Across the water where it chafes and moans—
Across the water at its widest part—
Which wilt thou leap—oh, lady of brave heart?

Their smiling eyes have met—those eager two:
She looks at Claud, as questioning which to do:

He rides—reins in—looks down the torrent's course,
Pats the sleek neck of his sure-footed horse,—
Stops,—measures spaces with his eagle eye,
Tries a new track, and yet returns to try.
Sudden, while pausing at the very brink,
The damp leaf-covered ground appears to sink,
And the keen instinct of the wise dumb brute
Escapes the yielding earth, the slippery root;
With a wild effort as if taking wing
The monstrous gap he clears with one safe spring;
Reaches—(and barely reaches)—past the roar
Of the wild stream, the further lower shore,—
Scrambles—recovers—rears—and panting stands
Safe 'neath his master's nerveless trembling hands.

Oh! even while he leapt, his horrid thought
Was of the peril to that lady brought;
Oh! even while he leapt, her Claud looked back,
And shook his hand to warn her from the track.
In vain: the pleasant voice she loved so well
Feebly re-echoed through that dreadful dell,
The voice that was the music of her home
Shouted in vain across that torrent's foam.

He saw her pausing on the bank above;
Saw,—like a dreadful vision of his love,—
That dazzling dream stand on the edge of death:
Saw it—and stared—and prayed—and held his
     breath.
Bright shone the Autumn sun on wood and plain;
On the steed's glossy flanks and flowing mane;
On the wild silver of the rushing brook;
On his wife's smiling and triumphant look;
Bright waved against the sky her wind-tost plume,
Bright on her freshened cheek the healthy bloom,—
Oh! all bright things, how could ye end in doom?

Forward they leaped! They leaped—a colored
     flash
Of life and beauty. Hark! a sudden crash,—
Blent with that dreadful sound, a man's sharp cry,—
Prone,—'neath the crumbling bank,—the horse
     and lady lie!

The heart grows humble in an awe-struck grief;
Claud thinks not, dreams not, plans not her relief.
Strengthen him but, O God! to reach the place,

And let him look upon her dying face!
Let him but say farewell! farewell, sweet love!
And once more hear her speak, and see her move,—
And ask her if she suffers where she lies,--
And kiss the lids down on her closing eyes,—
And he will be content.

     He climbs and strives:
The strength is in his heart of twenty lives;
Across the leaf-strewn gaps he madly springs;
From branch to branch like some wild ape he
  swings;
Breasts, with hot effort, that cold rushing source
Of death and danger.   With a giant's force
His bleeding hands and broken nails have clung
Round the gnarled slippery roots above him hung,
And now he's near,—he sees her through the leaves;
But a new horrid fear his mind receives:
The steed! his hoofs may crush that angel head!
No, Claud,—her favorite is already dead,
One shivering gasp thro' limbs that now stretch
  out like lead.

He's with her! is he dying too? his blood

Beats no more to and fro; his abstract mood
Weighs like a nightmare; something, well he knows,
Is horrible,—and still the horror grows;
But what it is, or how it came to pass,
Or why he lies half fainting on the grass,
Or what he strove to clutch at in his fall,
Or why he had no power for help to call,
This is confused and lost.

                But Claud has heard
A sound like breathings from a sleeping bird
New-caged that day,—a weak disturbing sigh,
The whisper of a grief that cannot cry,—
Repeated, and then still; and then again
Repeated,—and a long low moan of pain.

The hunt is passing; through the arching glade
The hounds sweep on in flickering light and shade,
The cheery huntsman winds his rallying horn,
And voices shouting from his guests that morn
Keep calling, calling, "Claud, the hunt is o'er,
Return we to the merry halls once more!"
Claud hears not; heeds not;—all is like a dream,
Except that lady lying by the stream;

Above all tumult of uproarious sound
Comes the faint sigh that breathes along the ground,
Where pale as death in her returning life
Writhes the sweet angel whom he still calls wife.

He parts the masses of her golden hair,
He lifts her, helpless, with a shuddering care,
He looks into her face with awe-struck eyes;—
She dies—the darling of his soul—she dies!

You might have heard, through that thought's
        fearful shock,
The beating of his heart like some huge clock;
And then the strong pulse falter and stand still,
When lifted from that fear with sudden thrill
He bent to catch faint murmurs of his name,
Which from those blanched lips low and trembling
        came;
"Oh! Claud!" she said: no more—

                        But never yet,
Through all the loving days since first they met,
Leaped his heart's blood with such a yearning vow
That she was all in all to him, as now.

"Oh! Claud—the pain!"

           "Oh! Gertrude, my beloved!'"

Then faintly o'er her lips a wan smile moved,
Which dumbly spoke of comfort from his tone,
As though she felt half saved, not so to die alone.

Ah! happy they who in their grief or pain
Yearn not for some familiar face in vain;
Who in the sheltering arms of love can lie
Till human passion breathes its latest sigh;
Who, when words fail to enter the dull ear,
And when eyes cease from seeing forms most dear,
Still the fond clasping touch can understand,—
And sink to death from that detaining hand!

He sits and watches; and she lies and moans;
The wild stream rushes over broken stones;
The dead leaves flutter to the mossy earth;
Far-away echoes bring the hunters' mirth;
And the long hour creeps by—too long—too long
Till the chance music of a peasant's song
Breaks the hard silence with a human hope,
And Claud starts up and gazes down the slope;

And from a wandering herdsman he obtains
The help whose want has chilled his anxious veins.
Into a simple litter then they bind
Thin cradling branches deftly intertwined ;
And there they lay the lady as they found her,
With all her bright hair streaming sadly round her
Her white lips parted o'er the pearly teeth
Like pictured saints', who die a martyr's death—
And slowly bear her, like a corse of clay,
Back to the home she left so blithe to-day.

The starry lights shine forth from tower and hall,
Stream through the gateway, glimmer on the wall,
And the loud pleasant stir of busy men
In courtyard and in stables sounds again.
And through the windows, as that death-bier passes,
They see the shining of the ruby glasses
Set at brief intervals for many a guest
Prepared to share the laugh, the song, the jest ;
Prepared to drink, with many a courtly phrase,
Their host and hostess—'Health to the Garayes!'
Health to the slender, lithe, yet stalwart frame
Of Claud Marot—Count of that noble name ;

Health to his lovely Countess : health—to her!

Scarce seems she now with faintest breath to stir

Oh! half-shut eyes—oh! brow with torture damp—

Will life's oil rise in that expiring lamp?

Are there yet days to come, or does he bend

Over a hope of which this is the end?

He shivers, and hot tears shut out the sight

Of that dear home for feasting made so bright;

The golden evening light is round him dying,

The dark rooks to their nests are slowly flying,

As underneath the portal, faint with fear,

He sees her carried, now so doubly dear;

"Save her!" is written in his anxious glances,

As the quick-summoned leech in haste advances.

"Save her!"—and through the gloom of midnight
      hours,

And through the hot noon, shut from air and
      flowers,

Young Claud sits patient—waiting day by day

For health for that sweet lady of Garaye.

The Lady of La Garaye.

PART II.

FIRST walk after sickness: the
    sweet breeze
That murmurs welcome in the
    bending trees,
When the cold shadowy foe of life
    departs,
And the warm blood flows freely thro' our hearts:
The smell of roses,—sound of trickling streams,
The elastic turf cross-barred with golden gleams,
That seems to lift, and meet our faltering tread;
The happy birds, loud singing over-head;
The glorious range of distant shade and light,
In blue perspective, rapturous to our sight,
Weary of draperied curtains folding round,

And the monotonous chamber's narrow bound;
With,—best of all,—the consciousness at length,
In every nerve, of sure returning strength :—

Long the dream stayed to cheer that darkened room,
That this should be the end of all that gloom!

Long, as the vacant life trained idly by,
She pressed her pillow with a restless sigh,—
" To-morrow, surely, I shall stronger feel!"
To-morrow! but the slow days onward steal,
And find her still with feverish aching head,
Still cramped with pain; still lingering in her bed;
Still sighing out the tedium of the time;
Still listening to the clock's recurring chime,
As though the very hours that struck were foes,
And might, but would not, grant complete repose.
Until the skilled physician—sadly bold
From frequent questioning—her sentence told!
That no good end could come to her faint yearn-
        ing,—
That no bright hour should see her health return-
        ing,—

That changeful seasons,—not for one dark year,
But on through life,—must teach her how to bear:
For through all Springs, with rainbow-tinted
    showers,
And through all Summers, with their wealth of
    flowers,
And every Autumn, with its harvest-home,
And all white Winters of the time to come,—
Crooked and sick forever she must be:
Her life of wild activity and glee
Was with the past;—the future was a life
Dismal and feeble; full of suffering; rife
With chill denials of accustomed joy,
Continual torment, and obscure annoy.
Blighted in all her bloom,—her withered frame
Must now inherit age; young but in name.
Never could she, at close of some long day
Of pain that strove with hope, exulting lay
A tiny new-born infant on her breast,
And, in the soft lamp's glimmer, sink to rest,
The strange corporeal weakness sweetly blent
With a delicious dream of full content;
With pride of motherhood, and thankful prayers"

And a confused glad sense of novel cares,

And peeps into the future brightly given,

As though her babe's blue eyes turned earth to
      heaven!

Never again could she, when Claud returned

After brief absence, and her fond heart yearned

To see his earnest eyes, with upward glancing,

Greet her known windows, even while yet ad-
      vancing,—

Fly with light footsteps down the great hall-stair,

And give him welcome in the open air,—

As though she were too glad to see him come,

To wait till he should enter happy home,—

And there, quick-breathing, glowing, sparkling
      stand,

His arm round her slim waist; hand locked in
      hand;

The mutual kiss exchanged of happy greeting,

That needs no secrecy of lovers' meeting;

While, giving welcome also in their way,

Her dogs barked rustling round him, wild with
      play;

And voices called, and hasty steps replied,

And the sleek fiery steed was led aside,
And the gray seneschal came forth and smiled,
Who held him in his arms while yet a child;
And cheery jinglings from unfastened doors,
And vaulted echoes through long corridors,
And distant bells that thrill along the wires,
And stir of logs that heap up autumn fires,
Crowned the glad eager bustle that makes known
The Master's step is on his threshold-stone!

Never again those rides so gladly shared,
So much enjoyed,—in which so much was dared
To prove no peril from the gate or brook,—
Need bring the shadow of an anxious look,
To mar the pleasant ray of proud surprise
That shone from out those dear protecting eyes.
No more swift hurrying through the summer rain,
That showered light silver on the freshened plain,
Hung on the tassels of the hazel bough,
And plashed the azure of the river's flow.
No more glad climbing of the mountain height,
From whence a map, drawn out in lines of light,
Showed dotting villages, and distant spires,

And the red rows of metal-burning fires,
And purple covering woods, within which stand
White mansions of the nobles of the land.

No more sweet wanderings far from tread of men,
In the deep thickets of the sunny glen,
To see the vanished Spring bud forth again;
Its well remembered tufts of primrose set
Among the sheltered banks of violet;
Or in thatched summer-houses sit and dream,
Through gurgling gushes of the woodland stream,
Then, rested, rise, and by the sunset ray
Saunter at will along the homeward way;
Pausing at each delight,—the singing loud
Of some sweet thrush, ere lingering eve be done;
Or the pink shining of some casual cloud
That blushes deeper as it nears the sun.

The rough wood-path; the little rocky burn;
Nothing of this can ever now return.
The life of joy is over: what is left
Is a half life; a life of strength bereft;
The body broken from the yearning soul,

Never again to make a perfect whole!
Helpless desires, and cravings unfulfilled;
Bitter regret, in stormy weepings stilled;
Strivings whose easy effort used to bless,
Grown full of danger and sharp weariness;
This is the life whose dreadful dawn must rise
When the night lifts, within whose gloom she lies:
Hope, on whose lingering help she leaned so late,
Struck from her clinging by the sword of fate—
The wild word NEVER, to her shrinking gaze,
Seems written on the wall in fiery rays.

Never!—our helpless changeful natures shrink
Before that word as from the grave's cold brink!
Set us a term whereto we must endure,
And you shall find our crown of patience sure;
But the irrevocable smites us down;—
Helpless we lie before the eternal frown;
Waters of Marah whelm the blinded soul,
Stifle the heart, and drown our self-control.
So, when she heard the grave physician speak,
Horror crept through her veins, who, faint and
          weak,

And tortured by all motion, yet had lain
With a meek cheerfulness that conquered pain,
Hoping,—till that dark hour.   Give back the hope,
Though years rise sad with intervening scope!
Scarce can those radiant eyes with sickly stare
Yet comprehend that sentence of despair:
Crooked and sick forever!   Crooked and sick!
She, in whose veins the passionate blood ran quick
As leaps the rivulet from the mountain height,
That dances rippling into Summer light;
She, in whose cheek the rich bloom always stayed,
And only deepened to a lovelier shade;
She, whose fleet limbs no exercise could tire,
When wild hill-climbing wooed her spirit higher!
Knell not above her bed this funeral chime;
Bid her be prisoner for a certain time;
Tell her blank years must waste in that changed
        home,
But not forever,—not for life to come;
Let infinite torture be her daily guest,
But set a term beyond which shall be rest.

In vain!   She sees that trembling fountain rise,

Tears of compassion in an old man's eyes:
And in low pitying tones, again he tells
The doom that sounds to her like funeral bells.
Long on his face her wistful gaze she kept;
Then dropped her head, and wildly moaned and
  wept;
Shivering through every limb, as lightning thought
Smote her with all the endless ruin wrought.
Never to be a mother!   Never give
Another life beyond her own to live,
Never to see her husband bless their child,
Thinking (dear blessèd thought!) like him it smiled:
Never again with Claud to walk or ride,
Partake his pleasures with a playful pride,
But cease from all companionship so shared,
And only have the hours his pity spared.
His pity—ah! his pity, would it prove
As warm and lasting as admiring love?
Or would her petty joys' late-spoken doom
Carry the great joy with them to joy's tomb?
Would all the hopes of life at once take wing?
The thought went through her with a secret sting,
And she repeated, with a moaning cry,

"Better to die, O God! 'Twere best to die!"
But we die not by wishing; in God's hour,
And not our own, do we yield up the power
To suffer or enjoy. The broken heart
Creeps through the world, encumbered by its clay;
While dearly loved and cherished ones depart,
Though prayer and sore lamenting clog their way.

She lived: she left that sick-room, and was brought
Into the scenes of customary thought:
The banquet-room, where lonely sunshine slept,
Saw her sweet eyes look round before she wept;
The garden heard the slow wheels of her chair,
When noon-day heat had warmed the untried air;
The pictures she had smiled upon for years,
Met her gaze trembling through a mist of tears;
Her favorite dog, his long unspoken name
Hearing once more, with timid fawning came;
It seemed as if all things partook her blight,
And sank in shadow like a spell of night.

And she saw Claud,—Claud in the open day,
Who through dim sunsets, curtained half away,

And by the dawn, and by the lamp's pale ray,
So long had watched her!

And Claud also saw,
That beauty which was once without a flaw;
And flushed,—but strove to hide the sense of
    shock,—
The feelings that some witchcraft seemed to mock.
Are those her eyes, those eyes so full of pain?
Her restless looks that hunt for ease in vain?
Is that her step, that halt uneven tread?
Is that her blooming cheek, so pale and dead?
Is that,—the querulous anxious mind that tells
Its little ills, and on each ailment dwells,—
The spirit alert which early morning stirred
Even as it rouses every gladsome bird,
Whose chorus of irregular music goes
Up with the dew that leaves the sun-touched rose?

Oh! altered, altered; even the smile is gone,
Which, like a sunbeam, once exulting shone!
Smiles have returned; but not the smiles of yore;
The joy, the youth, the triumph, are no more.
An anxious smile remains, that disconnects

Smiling from gladness; one that more dejects,
Than floods of passionate weeping, for it tries
To contradict the question of our eyes;
We say, "Thou'rt pained, poor heart, and full of
       woe?"
It drops that shining veil, and answers "No;"
Shrinks from the touch of unaccepted hands,
And while it grieves, a show of joy commands.
Wan shine such smiles;—as evening sunlight falls
On a deserted house whose empty walls
No longer echo to the children's play,
Or voice of ruined inmates fled away;
Where wintry winds alone, with idle state,
Move the slow swinging of its rusty gate.

But something sadder even than her pain
Torments her now, and thrills each languid vein.
Love's tender instinct feels through every nerve
When love's desires, or love itself doth swerve.
All the world's praise re-echoed to the sky
Cancels not blame that shades a lover's eye;
All the world's blame, which scorn for scorn repays,
Fails to disturb the joy of lover's praise.

Ah! think not vanity alone doth deck
With rounded pearls the young girl's innocent neck,
Who in her duller days contented tries
The homely robe that with no rival vies,
But on the happy night she hopes to meet
The one to whom she comes with trembling feet.
With crimson roses decks her bosom fair,
Warm as the thoughts of love all glowing there,
Because she must his favorite colors wear;
And all the bloom and beauty of her youth
Can scarce repay, she thinks, her lover's truth.

Vain is the argument so often moved,
"Who feels no jealousy hath never loved;"
She whose quick fading comes before her tomb,
Is jealous even of her former bloom.
Restless she pines; because, to her distress,
One charm the more is now one claim the less
On his regard whose words are her chief treasures,
And by whose love alone her worth she measures

Gertrude of La Garaye, thy heart is sore;
A worm is gnawing at the rose's core,

A doubt corrodeth all thy tender trust,

The freshness of thy day is choked in dust,

Not for the pain—although the pain be great,

Not for the change—though changed be all thy
    state ;

But for a sorrow dumb and unrevealed,

Most from its cause with mournful care concealed—

From Claud—who goes and who returns with sighs,

And gazes on his wife with wistful eyes,

And muses in his brief and cheerless rides

If her dull mood will mend ; and inly chides

His own sad spirit, that sinks down so low,

Instead of lifting her from all her woe ;

And thinks if he but loved her less, that he

Could cheer her drooping soul with gayety—

But wonders evermore that beauty's loss

To such a soul should seem so sore a cross.

Until one evening in that quiet hush

That lulls the falling day, when all the gush

Of various sounds seems buried with the sun,

He told his thought.

        As winter streamlets run,

Freed by some sudden thaw, and swift make way
Into the natural channels where they play,
So leaped her young heart to his tender tone,
So, answering to his warmth, resumed her own;
And all her doubt and all her grief confest,
Leaning her faint head on his faithful breast.

"Not always, Claud, did I my beauty prize;
Thy words first made it precious in my eyes,
And till thy fond voice made the gift seem rare,
Nor tongue nor mirror taught me I was fair.
I recked no more of beauty in that day
Of happy girlishness and childlike play,
Than some poor woodland bird, who stays his
    flight
On some low bough when summer days are bright,
And in that pleasant sunshine sits and sings,
And beaks the plumage of his glistening wings,
Recks of the passer-by who stands to praise
His feathered smoothness and his thrilling lays.
But now, I make my moan—I make my moan—
I weep the brightness lost, the beauty gone;
Because, now, fading is to fall from thee,

As the dead fruit falls blighted from the tree;
For thee,—not vanished loveliness,—I weep;
My beauty was a spell, thy love to keep;
For I have heard and read how men forsake
When time and tears that gift of beauty take,
Nor care although the heart they leave may break!"

A husband's love was there—a husband's love,—
Strong, comforting, all other loves above;
On her bowed neck he laid his tender hand,
And his voice steadied to his soul's command:
"Oh! thou mistaken and unhappy child,
Still thy complainings, for thy words are wild.
Thy beauty, though so perfect, was but one
Of the bright ripples dancing to the sun,
Which, from the hour I hoped to call thee wife,
Glanced down the silver stream of happy life.
Whatever change Time's heavy clouds may make,
Those are the waters which my thirst shall slake:
River of all my hopes thou wert and art;
The current of thy being bears my heart;
Whether it sweep along in shine or shade,
By barren rocks, or banks in flowers arrayed,

Foam with the storm, or glide in soft repose,—
In that deep channel, love unswerving flows!
How canst thou dream of beauty as a thing
On which depends the heart's own withering?
Lips budding red with tints of vernal years,
And delicate lids of eyes that shed no tears,
And light that falls upon the shining hair
As though it found a second sunbeam there,—
These must go by, my Gertrude, must go by;
The leaf must wither and the flower must die:
The rose can only have a rose's bloom;
Age would have wrought thy wondrous beauty's
      doom;
A little sooner did that beauty go—
A little sooner. Darling, take it so;
Nor add a strange despair to all this woe;
And take my faith, by changes unremoved,
To thy last hour of age and blight, beloved!"

But she again,—" Alas! not from distrust
I mourn, dear Claud, nor yet to thee unjust.
I love thee: I believe thee: yea, I know
Thy very soul is wrung to see my woe;

The earthquake of compassion trembles still
Within its depths, and conquers natural will.
But after,—after,—when the shock is past,—
When cruel Time, who flies to change so fast,
Hath made my suffering an accustomed thing,
And only left me slowly withering;
Then will the empty days rise chill and lorn,
The lonely evening, the unwelcome morn,
Until thy path at length be brightly crost
By some one holding all that I have lost;
Some one with youthful eyes, enchanting, bright,
Full as the morning of a liquid light;
And while my pale lip stiff and sad remains,
Her smiles shall thrill like sunbeams through thy
      veins:
I shall fade down, and she, with simple art,
All bloom and beauty, dance into thy heart!
Then, then, my Claud, shall I—at length alone—
Recede from thee with an unnoticed moan,
Sink where none heed me, and be seen no more,
Like waves that fringe the Netherlandish shore,
Which roll unmurmuring to the flat low land,
And sigh to death in that monotonous sand."

Again his earnest hand on hers he lays,
With love and pain and wonder in his gaze.

'Oh, darling! bitter word and bitter thought
What dæmon to thy trusting heart hath brought?
It may be thus within some sensual breast,
By passion's fire, not true love's power possest;
The creature love, that never lingers late,
A springtide thirst for some chance-chosen mate.
Oh! my companion, 'twas not so with me;
Not in the days long past, nor now shall be.
The drunken dissolute hour of Love's sweet cup,
When eyes are wild, and mantling blood is up,
Even in my youth to me was all unknown:
Until I truly loved, I was alone.
I asked too much of intellect and grace,
To pine, though young, for every pretty face,
Whose passing brightness to quick fancies made
A sort of sunshine in the idle shade;
Beauties who starred the earth like common flowers,
The careless eglantines of wayside bowers.
I lingered till some blossom rich and rare
Hung like a glory on the scented air,

Enamoring at once the heart and eye,

So that I paused, and could not pass it by.

Then woke the passionate love within my heart,

And only with my life shall that depart;

'Twas not so sensual strong, so loving weak,

To ebb when ebbs the rose-tinge on thy cheek;

Fade with thy fading, weakening day by day

Till thy locks silver with a dawning gray:

No, Gertrude, trust me, for thou mayst believe,

A better faith is that which I receive;

Sacred I'll hold the sacred name of wife,

And love thee to the sunset verge of life!

Yea, shall so much of empire o'er man's soul

Live in a wanton's smile, and no control

Bind down his heart to keep a steadier faith,

For links that are to last from life to death?

Let those who can, in transient loves rejoice,—

Still to new hopes breathe forth successive sighs,—

Give me the music of the accustomed voice,

And the sweet light of long familiar eyes!"

He ceased. But she, for all his fervent speech,

Sighed as she listened. "Claud, I cannot reach

The summit of the hope where thou wouldst set me,
And all I crave is, never to forget me!
Wedded I am to pain, and not to thee;
Thy life's companion I no more can be be,
For thou remainest all thou wert—but I
Am a fit bride for Death, and long to die.
Yea, long for death; for thou wouldst miss me then
More even than now, in mountain and in glen;
And musing by the white tomb where I lay,
Think of the happier time and earlier day,
And wonder if the love another gave
Equalled the passion buried in that grave."

Then with a patient tenderness he took
That pale wife in his arms, with yearning look:
"Oh! dearer now than when thy girlish tongue
Faltered consent to love while both were young,
Weep no more foolish tears, but lift thy head;
Those drops fall on my heart like molten lead;
And all my soul is full of vain remorse,
Because I let thee take that dangerous course,
Share in the chase, pursue with horn and hound,
And follow madly o'er the roughening ground.

5

Not lightly did I love, nor lightly choose;

Whate'er thou losest I will also lose;

If bride of Death,—being first my chosen bride,—

I will await death, lingering by thy side ;

And God, He knows, who reads all human thought,

And by whose will this bitter hour was brought,

How eagerly, could human pain be shifted,

I would lie low, and thou once more be lifted

To walk in beauty as thou didst before,

And smile upon the welcome world once more.

Oh! loved even to the brim of love's full fount,

Wilt thou set nothing to firm faith's account?

Choke back thy tears which are my bitter smart,

Lean thy dear head upon my aching heart;

It may be God, who saw our careless life,

Not sinful, yet not blameless, my sweet wife,

(Since all we thought of, in our youth's bright

     May,

Was but the coming joy from day to day,)

Hath blotted out all joy to bid us learn

That this is not our home; and make us turn

From the enchanted earth, where much was given,

To higher aims, and a forgotten heaven."

So spoke her love—and wept in spite of words;
While her heart echoed all his heart's accords,
And leaning down, she said with whispering sigh,
" I sinned, my Claud, in wishing so to die."
Then they, who oft in Love's delicious bowers
Had fondly wasted glad and passionate hours,
Kissed with a mutual moan :—but o'er their lips
Love's light passed clear, from under Life's eclipse.

The Lady of La Garaye.

OW Memory haunts us! When we
    fain would be
Alone and free,—
Uninterrupted by his mournful words,
Faint, indistinct, as are a wind-harp's
    chords
Hung on a leafless tree,—
He will not leave us: we resolve in vain
To chase him forth—for he returns again,
Pining incessantly!
In the old pathways of our lost delights
He walks on sunny days and starlit nights,
Answering our restless moan,
With,—"I am here alone,

My brother Joy is gone—forever gone!
Round your decaying home
The Spring indeed is come,
The leaves are thrilling with a sense of life,
The sap of flowers is rife,
But where is Joy, Heaven's messenger,—bright
      Joy,—
That curled and radiant boy,
Who was the younger brother of my heart?
Why let ye him whom I so loved depart?
Call him once more,
And let us all be glad, as heretofore!"

Then, urged and stung by Memory, we go forth,
And wander south and north,
Deeming Joy yet may answer to our yearning;
But all is blank and bare:
The silent air
Echoes no pleasant shout of his returning.
Yet somewhere—somewhere, by the pathless
      woods,
Or silver rippling floods,
He wanders as he wandered once with us;

Through bright arcades of cities populous;
Or else in deserts rude,
Happy in solitude,
And choosing only Youth to be his mate,
He leaves us to our fate.
We hear his distant laughter as we go,
Pacing, ourselves, with Woe,—
But us he hath outstripped for evermore!
Seek him not in the wood,
Where the sweet ring-doves ever murmuring
      brood;
Nor on the hill, nor by the golden shore;
Others inherit that which once was ours;
The freshness of the hours,—
The sparkling of the early morning rime,
The evanescent glory of the time!

With them, in some sweet glade,
Warm with a summer shade,
Or where white clover, blooming fresh and wild,
Breathes like the kisses of a little child,
He lingers now :—we call him back in vain
To our world's snow and rain ;

The bower we built him when he was our guest
Life's storms have beaten down,
And he far off hath flown,
And buildeth where there is a sunnier nest;
Or, closing rainbow wings and laughing eyes,
He lieth basking 'neath the open skies,
Taking his rest
On the soft moss of some unbroken ground,
Where sobs did never sound.
Oh! give him up: confess that Joy has gone :
He met you at the source of Life's bright river :
And if he hath passed on,
'Tis that his task is done,
He hath no future meseage to deliver,
But leaves you lone and still forever and forever !

PART III.

EVER again! When first that sentence fell
From lips so loth the bitter truth to tell,
Death seemed the balance of its burdening care,
The only end of such a strange despair.
To live deformed; enfeebled; still to sigh
Through changeless days, that o'er the heart go by
Colorless,—formless,—melting as they go
Into a dull and unrecorded woe,—
Why strive for galdness in such dreary shade?
Why seek to feel less cheerless, less afraid?
What recks a little more or less of gloom,

When a continual darkness is our doom?
But custom,—which, to unused eyes that dwell
Long in the blankness of a prison cell,
At length shows glimmerings through some ruined
      hole,—
Trains to endurance the imprisoned soul;
And teaching how with deepest gloom to cope,
Bids patience light her lamp, when sets the sun
      of hope.

And even like one who sinks to brief repose
Cumbered with mournfulness from many woes;
Who, restless dreaming, full of horror sleeps,
And with a worse than waking anguish weeps,
Till in his dream some precipice appear
Which he must face, however great his fear:
Who stepping on those rocks, then feels them break
Beneath him,—and, with shrieks, leaps up awake;
And seeing but the gray unwelcome morn,
And feeling but the usual sense forlorn
Of loss and dull remembrance of known grief,
Melts into tears that partly bring relief,
Because, though misery holds him, yet his dreams

More dreadful were than all around him seems:—
So, in the life grown real of loss and woe,
She woke to crippled days; which, sad and slow
And infinitely weary as they were,
At first appeared less hard than fancy deemed, to
     bear.
But as those days rolled on, of grinding pain,
Of wild untamed regrets, and yearnings vain,
Sad Gertrude grew to weep with restless tears
For all the vanished joys of blighted years.
And most she mourned with feverish piteous
     pining,
When o'er the land the summer sun was shining;
And all the volumes and the missals rare,
Which Claud had gathered with a tender care,
Seemed nothing to the book of nature, spread
Around her helpless feet and weary head.

Oh! woodland paths she ne'er again may see;
Oh! tossing branches of the forest tree;
Oh! loveliest banks in all the land of France,
Glassing your shadows in the silvery Rance;
Oh! river with your swift yet quiet tide,

Specked with white sails that seem in dreams tc
      glide;
Oh! ruddy orchards, basking on the hills,
Whose plenteous fruit the thirsty flagon fills;
And oh! ye winds, which, free and unconfined,
No sickness poisons, and no heart can bind,—
Restore her to enjoyment of the earth!
Echo again her songs of careless mirth,
Those little Breton songs so wildly sweet,
Fragments of music strange and incomplete,
Her small red mouth went warbling by the way
Through the glad roamings of her active day.

It may not be!   Blighted are summer hours!
The bee goes booming through the plats of flowers,
The butterfly its tiny mate pursues
With rapid fluttering of its painted hues,
The thin-winged gnats their transient time employ
Reeling through sunbeams in a dance of joy,
The small field-mouse with wide transparent ears
Comes softly forth, and softly disappears,
The dragon-fly hangs glittering on the reed,
The spider swings across his filmy thread,

And gleaming fishes, darting to and fro,
Make restless silver in the pools below.
All these poor lives—these lives of small account,
Feel the ethereal thrill within them mount;
But the great human life,—the life Divine,—
Rests in dull torture, heavy and supine,
And the bird's song, by Garaye's walls of stone,
Crosses within, the irrepressible moan!
The slow salt tears, half weakness and half grief,
That sting the eyes before they bring relief,
And which with weary lids she strives in vain
To prison back upon her aching brain,
Fall down the lady's cheek,—her heart is breaking:
A mournful sleep is hers; a hopeless waking;
And oft, in spite of Claud's beloved rebuke,
When first the awful wish her spirit shook,—
She dreams of DEATH,—and of that quiet shore
In the far world where eyes shall weep no more,
And where the soundless feet of angels pass
With floating lightness o'er the sea of glass.

Nor is she sole in gloom. Claud too hath lost
His power to soothe her,—all his thoughts are tost

As in a storm of sadness: shall he speak
To her, who lies so faint, and lone, and weak,
Of pleasant walks and rides? or yet describe
The merry sayings of that careless tribe
Of friends and boon companions now unseen,—
Or the wild beauty of the forest green,—
Or daring feats and hair-breadth 'scapes, which they
Who are not crippled, think a thing for play?

He dare not:—oft without apparent cause
He checks his speaking with a faltering pause;
Oft when she bids him, with a mournful smile,
By stories such as these the hour beguile,
And he obeys—only because she bids—
He sees the large tears welling 'neath the lids.
Or if a moment's gayety return
To his young heart, that scarce can yet unlearn
Its habits of delight in all things round,
And he grows eager on some subject found
In their discourse, linked with the outward world,
Till with a pleasant smile his lip is curled,—
Even with her love she smites him back to pain!
Upon his hand her tears and kisses rain;

And with a suffocated voice she cries,
"O! Claud—the old bright days!"

                    And then he sighs,
And with a wistful heart makes new endeavor
To cheer or to amuse ;—and so forever,
Till in his brain the grief he tries to cheat,
A dreary mill-wheel circling seems to beat,
And drive out other thoughts—all thoughts but one
That he and she are both alike undone,—
That better were their mutual fate, if when
That leap was taken in the fatal glen,
Both had been found, released from pain and dread,
In the rough waters of the torrent's bed,
And greeted pitying eyes, with calm smiles of the
      Dead!

A spell is on the efforts each would make,
With willing spirit, for the other's sake :
Through some new path of thought he fain would
      move,—
And she her languid hours would fain employ;
But bitter grows the sweetness of their love,—
And a lament lies under all their joy.

She watches Claud,—bending above the page;
Thinks him grown pale, and wearying with his care;
And with a sigh his promise would engage
For happy exercise and summer air:
He watches her, as sorrowful she lies,
And thinks she dreams of woman's hope denied;
Of the soft gladness of a young child's eyes,
And pattering footsteps on the terrace wide,—
Where sunshine sleeps, as in a home for light,
And glittering peacocks make a rainbow show,—
But which seems sad, because that terrace bright
Must evermore remain as lone as now.

And either tries to hide the thoughts that wring
Their secret hearts; and both essay to bring
Some happy topic, some yet lingering dream,
Which they with cheerful words shall make their
     theme;
But fail,—and in their wistful eyes confess
All their words never own of hopelessness.

Was then DESPAIR the end of all this woe?
Far off the angel voices answer, No!

Devils despair, for they believe and tremble;
But man believes and hopes.   Our griefs resemble
Each other but in this.   Grief comes from Heaven;
Each thinks his own the bitterest trial given;
Each wonders at the sorrows of his lot;
His neighbor's sufferings presently forgot,
Though wide the difference which our eyes can see
Not only in grief's kind, but its degree.
God grants to some, all joys for their possession,
Nor loss, nor cross, the favored mortal mourns;
While some toil on, outside those bounds of blessing,
Whose weary feet forever tread on thorns.
But over all our tears God's rainbow bends;
To all our cries a pitying ear He lends;
Yea, to the feeble sound of man's lament
How often have His messengers been sent!
No barren glory circles round His throne,
By mercy's errands were his angels known;
Where hearts were heavy, and where eyes were
        dim,
There did the brightness radiate from Him;
God's pity,—clothed in an apparent form,—
Starred with a polar light the human storm,

Floated o'er tossing seas man's sinking bark,
And for all dangers built one sheltering ark.

When a slave's child lay dying, parched with thirst,
Till o'er the arid waste a fountain burst,—
When Abraham's mournful hand upheld the knife
To smite the silver cord of Isaac's life,—
When faithful Peter in his prison slept,—
When lions to the feet of Daniel crept,—
When the tried Three walked thro' the furnace glare,
Believing God was with them, even there,—
When to Bethesda's sunrise-smitten wave
Poor trembling cripples crawled their limbs to lave:
In all the various forms of human trial,
Brimming that cup, filled from a bitter vial,
Which even the suffering Christ with fainting cry
Under God's will had shudderingly passed by :—
To hunger, pain, and thirst, and human dread;
Imprisonment; sharp sorrow for the dead;
Deformed contraction; burdensome disease;
Humbling and fleshly ill!—to all of these
The shining messengers of comfort came,—
God's angels,—healing in God's holy name.

And when the crowning pity sent to earth
The Man of Sorrows, in mysterious birth;
And the angelic tones with one accord
Made loving chorus to proclaim the Lord;
Was Isaac's guardian there, and he who gave
Hagar the sight of that cool gushing wave?
Did the defender of the youthful Three,
And Peter's usher, join that psalmody?
With him who at the dawn made healing sure,
Troubling the waters with a freshening cure;
And those, the elect, to whom the task was given
To offer solace to the Son of Heaven,
When,—mortal tremors by the Immortal felt,—
Pale, 'neath the Syrian olives, Jesu knelt,
Alone,—'midst sleeping followers warned in vain;
Alone with God's compassion, and His pain!

Cease we to dream. Our thoughts are yet more dim
Than children's are, who put their trust in Him.
All that our wisdom knows, or ever can,
Is this: that God hath pity upon man;
And where His Spirit shines in Holy Writ,
The great word Comforter comes after it.

The Lady of La Garaye.

PART IV.

ILENT old gateway! whose two col-
    umns stand
  Like simple monuments on either
    hand;
  No trellised iron-work, with pleasant
    view
Of trim-set flowery gardens shining through;
No bolts to bar unasked intruders out;
No well-oiled hinge whose sound, like one low note
Of music, tells the listening hearts that yearn,
Expectant of dear footsteps, where to turn;
No ponderous bell whose loud vociferous tone
Into the rose-decked lodge hath echoing gone,
Bringing the porter forth with brief delay,

To spread those iron wings that check the way;
Nothing but ivy-leaves, and crumbling stone;
Silent old gateway,—even *thy* life is gone!

But ere those columns, lost in ivied shade,
Black on the midnight sky their forms portrayed;
And ere thy gate, by damp weeds overtopped,
Swayed from its rusty fastenings and then dropped,
When it stood portal to a living home,
And saw the living faces go and come,
What various minds, and in what various moods,
Crossed the fair paths of these sweet solitudes!

Old gateway, thou hast witnessed times of mirth,
When light the hunter's gallop beat the earth;
When thy quick wakened echo could but know
Laughter and happy voices, and the flow
Of jocund spirits, when the pleasant sight
Of broidered dresses (careless youth's delight)
Trooped by at sunny morn, and back at falling night.

And thou hast witnessed triumph,—when the Bride
Passed through, the stately Bridegroom at her side;

The village maidens scattering many a flower,
Bright as the bloom of living beauty's dower,
With cheers and shouts that bid the soft tears rise
Of joy exultant, in her downcast eyes.
And thou hadst gloom, when,—fallen from beauty's
      state,—
Her mournful litter rustled through the gate,
And the wind waved its branches as she passed,—
And the dishevelled curls around her cast,
Rose on that breeze and kissed, before they fell,
The iron scroll-work with a wild farewell!

And thou hast heard sad dirges chanted low,
And sobbings loud from those who saw with woe
The feet borne forward by a funeral train,
Which homeward never might return again,
Nor in the silence of the frozen nights
Reclaim that dwelling and its lost delights;
But lowly lie, however wild love's yearning,
The dust that clothed them, unto dust returning.
Through thee, how often hath been borne away
Man's share of dual life—the senseless clay!
Through thee, how oft hath hastened, glad and bold,

God's share—the eager spirit in that mould ;
But neither life nor death hath left a trace
On the strange silence of that vacant place.

Not vacant in the day of which I write!
Then rose thy pillared columns fair and white;
Then floated out the odorous pleasant scent
Of cultured shrubs and flowers together blent,
And o'er the trim-kept gravel's tawny hue
Warm fell the shadows and the brightness too.

Count Claud is at the gate, but not alone :
Who is his friend?

          They pass, and both are gone.
Gone, by the bright warm path, to those sad halls
Where now his slackened step in sadness falls ;
Sadness of every day and all day long,
Spite of the summer glow and wild-bird's song.

Who is that slow-paced Priest to whom he bows
Courteous precedence, as he sighing shows
The oriel window where his Gertrude dwells,
And all her mournful story briefly tells?

Who is that friend whose hand with gentle clasp
Answers his own young agonizing grasp,
And looks upon his burst of passionate tears
With calmer grieving of maturer years?

Oh! well round that friend's footsteps might be
     breathed
The blessing which the Italian poet wreathed
Into a garland gay of graceful words
As full of music as a lute's low chords;
"Blessed be the year, the time, the day, the hour,"
When He passed through those gates, whose gentle
     power
Lifted with ministrant zeal the leaden grief,
Probed the soul's festering wounds and brought
     relief,
And taught the sore vexed spirits where to find
Balm that could heal, and thoughts that cheered
     the mind.

Prior of Benedictines, did thy prayers
Bring down a blessing on them unawares,
While yet their faces were to thee unknown,

And thou wert kneeling in thy cell alone,
Where thy meek litanies went up to Heaven,
That ALL who suffered might have comfort given,
And thy heart yearned for all thy fellow-men,
Smitten with sorrows far beyond thy ken?

He sits by Gertrude's couch, and patient listens
To her wild grieving voice;—his dark eye glistens
With tearful sympathy for that young wife,
Telling the torture of her broken life;
And when he answers her she seems to know
The peace of resting by a river's flow.
Tender his words, and eloquently wise;
Mild the pure fervor of his watchful eyes;
Meek with serenity of constant prayer
The luminous forehead, high and broad and bare;
The thin mouth, though not passionless, yet still;
With a sweet calm that speaks an angel's will,
Resolving service to his God's behest,
And ever musing how to serve Him best.
Not old, nor young; with manhood's gentlest grace;
Pale to transparency the pensive face,
Pale not with sickness, but with studious thought,

The body tasked, the fine mind overwrought;
With something faint and fragile in the whole,
As though 'twere but a lamp to hold a soul.
Such was the friend who came to La Garaye,
And Claud and Gertrude lived to bless the day!

There is a love that hath not lover's wooing,
Love's wild caprices, nor love's hot pursuing;
But yet a clinging and persistent love,
Tenderly binding, most unapt to rove;
As full of fervent and adoring dreams,
As the more gross and earthlier passion seems,
But far more single-hearted; from its birth,
With humblest notions of unequal worth!
Guided and guidable; with thankful trust;
Timid, lest all complaint should be unjust;
Circling,—a lesser orb,—around its star
With tributary love, that dare not war.
Such is the love which aged men inspire;
Priests, whose pure hearts are full of sacred fire;
And friends of dear friends dead,—whom trembling
        we admire.
A touch of mystery lights the rising morn

Of love for those who lived ere we were born;
Whose eyes the eyes of ancestors have seen;
Whose voice hath answered voices that have been;
Whose words show wisdom gleaned in days gone by,
As glory flushes from a sunset sky.
Our judgment leans upon them, feeling weak;
Our hearts lift yearning towards them as they
        speak,
And silently we listen, lest we lose
Some teaching truth, and benefits refuse.

With such a love did Gertrude learn to greet
The gentle Prior; whose slow-pacing feet
Each day of her sad life made welcome sound
Across the bright path of her garden ground.
And ere the golden summer passed away,
And leaves were yellowing with a pale decay;
Ere, drenched by sweeping storms of autumn rain,
In turbulent billows lay the beaten grain;
Ere Breton orchards, ripening, turn to red
All the green freshness which the spring-time shed,
Mocking the glory which the sunset fills
With stripes of crimson o'er the painted hills, —

Her thoughts submitted to his thoughts' control,
As 'twere an elder brother of her soul.

Well she remembered how that soul was stirred,
By the rebuking of his gentle word,
When in her faltering tones complaint was given,
"What had I done, to earn such fate from Heaven?"

"O, Lady! here thou liest, with all that wealth
Or love can do to cheer thee back to health;
With books that woo the fancies of thy brain,
To happier thoughts than brooding over pain;
With light, with flowers, with freshness, and with
        food,
Dainty and chosen, fit for sickly mood;
With easy couches for thy languid frame,
Bringing real rest, and not the empty name;
And silent nights, and soothed and comforted days;
And Nature's beauty spread before thy gaze:—

"What have the Poor done, who instead of these,
Suffer in foulest rags each dire disease,
Creep on the earth, and lean against the stones,

When some disjointing torture racks their bones;
And groan and grope throughout the weary night,
Denied the rich man's easy luxury—light?
What has the Babe done,—who with tender eyes,
Blinks at the world a little while, and dies,
Having first stretched in wild convulsive leaps
His fragile limbs, which ceaseless suffering keeps
In ceaseless motion, till the hour when death
Clenches his little heart, and stops his breath?
What has the Idiot done, whose half-formed soul
Scarce knows the seasons as they onward roll;
Who flees with gibbering cries, and bleeding feet,
From idle boys who pelt him in the street?
What have the fair girls done, whose early bloom
Wasting like flowers that pierce some creviced
       tomb,
Plants that have only known a settled shade,
Lives that for others' uses have been made,—
Toil on from morn to night, from night to morn,
For those chance pets of Fate, the wealthy born;
Bound not to murmur, and bound not to sin,
However bitter be the bread they win?
What hath the Slandered done, who vainly strives

To set his life among untarnished lives?
Whose bitter cry for justice only fills
The myriad echoes lost among life's hills;
Who hears for evermore the self-same lie
Clank clog-like at his heel when he would try
To climb above the loathly creeping things
Whose venom poisons, and whose fury stings,
And so slides back; forever doomed to hear
The old witch, Malice, hiss with serpent leer
The old hard falsehood to the old bad end,
Helped, it may be, by some traducing friend,
Or one rocked with him on one mother's breast,—
Learned in the art of where to smite him best.

" What we must suffer, proves not what was done :
So taught the God of Heaven's anointed Son,
Touching the blind man's eyes amid a crowd
Of ignorant seething hearts, who cried aloud,
The blind, or else his parents, had offended :
That was Man's preaching; God that preaching
          mended.
But whatsoe'er we suffer, being still
Fixed and appointed by the heavenly will,

Behooves us bear with patience as we may
The Potter's moulding of our helpless clay.
Much, Lady, hath He taken, but He leaves
What outweighs all for which thy spirit grieves;
No greater gift lies even in God's control
Than the large love that fills the human soul.
If, taking that, He left thee all the rest,
Would not vain anguish wring thy pining breast?
If, taking all, that dear love yet remains,
Hath it not balm for all thy bitter pains?

"Oh, Lady! there are lonely deaths that make
The heart that thinks upon them burn and ache;
And such I witnessed on the purple shore
Where scorched Vesuvius rears his summit hoar,
And Joan's gaunt palace, with its skull-like eyes,
And barbarous and cruel memories,
Forever sees the blue wave lap its feet,
Ana the white glancing of the fishers' fleet.
The death of the FORSAKEN! lone he lies,
His sultry noon, fretted by slow black flies,
That settle on pale cheek and quivering brow
With a soft torment.   The increasing glow

Brings the full shock of day; the hot air grows
Impure alike from action and repose;
Bruised fruit, and faded flowers, and dung and dust,
The rich man's stew-pan, and the beggar's crust,
Poison the faint lips opening hot and dry,
Loathing the plague they breathe with gasping sigh.
The thick oppression of its stifling heat,
The busy murmur of the swarming street,
The roll of chariots and the rush of feet;
With the tormenting music's nasal twang
Distorting melodies his loved ones sang!

"Then comes a change—not silence, but less sound,
Less echo of hard footsteps on the ground,
Less rolling thunder of vociferous words,
As though the clang struck out in crashing chords
Fell into single notes, that promise rest
To the wild fever of the laboring breast.

"Last cometh on the night—the hot, bad night,
With less of all—of heat, of dust, of light;
And leaves him watching, with a helpless stare,—
The theme of no one's hope and no one's care!

7

The cresset lamp, that stands so grim and tall,
Widens and wavers on the upper wall;
And calming down from day's perpetual storm,
His thoughts' dark chaos takes some certain form,
And he begins to pine for joys long lost,
Or hopes unrealized;—till bruised and tost
He sends his soul vain journeys through the gloom
For radiant eyes that should have wept his doom.
Then clasps his hands in prayer, and for a time,
Gives aspirations unto things sublime:
But sinking to some speck of sorrow found,
Some point which, like a little festering wound,
Holds all his share of pain,—he gazes round,
Seeking some vanished form, some hand whose touch
Would almost cure him; and he yearns so much,
That passionate painful sobs his breathing choke,
And the thin bubble of his dream hath broke!

"So, still again; and all alone again;
Not even a vision present with his pain.
The hot real round him; the forsaken bed;
The tumbled pillow and the restless head.
The drink so near his couch, and yet too far

For feeble hands to reach; the cold fine star
That glitters through the unblinded window-pane,
And with slow gliding leaves it blank again;
Till morning flushing through the world once more,
Brings the dull likeness of the day before,—
The first vague freshness of new wings unfurled,
As though Hope lighted, somewhere, in the world
The heat of noon; the fading down of light;
The glimmering evening, and the restless night.
And then again the morning;—and the noon;
The evening and the morning;—till a boon
Of double weakness sinks him, and he knows
One or two other days shall end his woes;
One or two mournful evenings, glimmering gray,
One or two hopeless risings of new day,
One or two noons too weak to brush off flies,
One or two nights of flickering feeble sighs,
One or two shivering breaks of helpless tears,
One or two yearnings for forgotten years,—
And then the end of all, then the great change,
When the freed soul, let loose at length to range,
Leaves the imprisoning and imprisoned clay,
And soars far out of reach of sorrow and decay!"

Then Claud, who watched the faint and pitying flush
Tint her transparent cheek, with sudden gush
Of manly ardor spoke of soldier deaths;
Of scattered slain who lay on cold bleak heaths;
Of prisoners pining for their native land
After the battle's vain and desperate stand;
Brave hearts in dungeons,—rusting like their
       swords;
And wounded men,—midst whom the rifling hordes
Of spoil-desiring searchers crept and smote,—
Who vainly heard the rallying bugle's note,
Or the quick march of their companions pass;
Sunk, dumb and dying, on the trampled grass.

Then also, the meek anxious Prior told
Of war's worst horrors,—when in freezing cold,
Or in the torrid heat, men lay and groaned,
With none to hear or heed them when they moaned;
Or, with half-help,—borne in a comrade's arms
To where, all huddled up in feverish swarms,
The dying numbers mocked the scanty skill
Of wearied surgeons,—crowding, crowding still
With different small degrees of lingering breath.

Asking for instant aid, or choked in death.
Order, and cleanliness, and thought, and care,
The hush of quiet, or the sound of prayer,
These things were not:—nor, from the exhausted
        store,
Medicines and balms, to help the troubling sore;
Nor soft cool lint, like dew on parched-up ground,
Clothing the weary, burning, festering wound;
Nor delicate linen; nor fresh cooling drinks
To woo the fever-cracking lip, which shrinks
Even from such solace; nor the presence blest
Of holy women watching broken rest,
And gliding past them through the wakeful night,
Like her whose Shadow made the soldier's light.'

And as the three discoursed of things like these,
Sweet Gertrude felt her mind grow ill at ease.
The words of Claud,—that God took what was
        given,
To teach their hearts to turn from earth to heaven;
The Prior's words, of tender mild appeal,
Teaching her how for others' woes to feel;
Weighed on her heart; till all the past life seemed

Thankless and thoughtless: and the lady dreamed
Of succor to the helpless, and of deeds
Pious and merciful, whose beauty breeds
Good deeds in others, copying what is done,
And ending all by earnest thought begun.

Nor idly dreamed.   Where once the shifting throng
Of merry playmates met, with dance and song,—
Long rows of simple beds the place proclaim
A Hospital, in all things but the name.
In that same castle where the lavish feast
Lay spread, that fatal night, for many a guest,
The sickly poor are fed!   Beneath that porch
Where Claud shed tears that seemed the lids to
        scorch,
Seeing her broken beauty carried by
Like a crushed flower that now has but to die,
The self-same Claud now stands and helps to guide
Some ragged wretch to rest and warmth inside.
But most to those, the hopeless ones, on whom,
Early or late, her own sad spoken doom
Hath been pronounced—the Incurables—she spends
Her lavish pity, and their couch attends.

Her home is made their home; her wealth their
     dole;
Her busy courtyard hears no more the roll
Of gilded vehicles, or pawing steeds,
But feeble steps of those whose bitter needs
Are their sole passport. Through that gateway
     press
All varying forms of sickness and distress,
And many a poor worn face that hath not smiled
For years,—and many a feebled crippled child,
Blesses the tall white portal where they stand,
And the dear Lady of the liberal hand.

Not in a day such happy change was brought:
Not in a day the works of mercy wrought:
But in God's gradual time. As Winter's chain
Melts from the earth and leaves it green again;
As the fresh bud a crimsoning beauty shows
From the black briers of a last year's rose;
So the full season of her love matures,
And her one illness breeds a thousand cures.
Her soft eyes looking into other eyes,
Bleared, and defaced to blinding cavities,

Weary not in their task; nor turn away
With a sick loathing from their glimmering ray.
Her small white comforting hand,—no longer hid
In pearl-embroidered gauntlet,—lifts the lid
Outworn with labor in the bitter fields,
And with a tender skill some healing yields;
Bathes the swollen redness,—shades unwelcome
　　　light,—
And into morning turns their threatening night.

And Claud, her eager Claud, with fervent heart,
Earnest in all things, nobly does his part;
His high intelligence hath mastered much
That baffled science: with a surgeon's touch
He treats,—himself,—the hurts from many a wound,
And, by deep study, novel cures hath found.
But good and frank and simple he remains,
Though a King's notice lauds successful pains;
And, echoing through his grateful country, fame
Sends to far nations noble Garaye's name.[2]
Oh! loved and reverenced long that name shall be,
Though, crumbled on the soil of Brittany,
No stone, at last, of that pale Ruin shows

Where stood the gateway of his joys and woes.
For, in the Breton town, the good deeds done
Yield a fresh harvest still, from sire to son;
Still thrives the noble Hospital that gave
Shelter to those whom none from pain could save :
Still to the Schools the ancient chiming clock
Calls the poor yeanlings of a simple flock;
Still the calm Refuge for the fallen and lost
(Whom love a blight and not a blessing crost,)
Sends out a voice to woo the grieving breast—
Come unto me, ye weary, and find rest!
And still the gentle Nurses,—vowed to give
Their aid to all who suffer and yet live,—
Go forth in snow-white cap and sable gown,
Tending the sick and hungry in the town,
And show dim pictures on their quiet walls
Of those who dwelt in Garaye's ruined halls!

CONCLUSION.

PEACE to their ashes! Far away
 they lie,
Among their poor, beneath the equal
 sky,—
Among their poor, who blessed them
 ere they went
For all the loving help and calm content.
Oh! happy beings, who have gone to hear
" Well done, ye faithful servants," sounding clear;
How easy all your virtues to admire!
How hard, alas! to copy and aspire!

Servant of God, well done! They serve God well,
Who serve his creatures: when the funeral bell

Tolls for the dead, there's nothing left of all
That decks the scutcheon and the velvet pall
Save this.   The coronet is empty show:
The strength and loveliness are hid below:
The shifting wealth to others hath accrued:
And learning cheers not the grave's solitude:
What's DONE, is what remains!   Ah, blessed they
Who leave completed tasks of love to stay
And answer mutely for them, being dead:
Life was not purposeless, though Life be fled.
Even as I write, before me seem to rise,
Like stars in darkness, well-remembered eyes
Whose light but lately shone on earth's endeavor,
Now vanished from this troubled world forever.
Oh! missed and mourned by many,—I being one,—
HERBERT, not vainly thy career was run;
Nor shall Death's shadow, and the folding shroud,
Veil from the future years thy worth allowed.
Since all thy life thy single hope and aim
Was to do good,—not make thyself a name,—
'Tis fit that by the good remaining yet,
Thy name be one men never can forget.
Oh! eyes I first knew in our mutual youth,

So full of limpid earnestness and truth;
Eyes I saw fading still, as day by day
The body, not the spirit's strength, gave way;
Eyes that I last saw lifting their farewell
To the now darkened windows where I dwell,—
And wondered, as I stood there sadly gazing,
If Death were brooding in their faint upraising;
If never more thy footstep light should cross
My threshold stone—but friends bewail thy loss,
And She be widowed young, who lonely trains
Children that boast thy good blood in their veins;
Fair eyes,—your light was quenched while men
      still thought
To see those tasks to full perfection brought!
But Good is not a shapely mass of stone,
Hewn by man's hands and worked by him alone;
It is a seed God suffers One to sow,—
Many to reap; and when the harvests grow,
God giveth increase through all coming years,—
And lets us reap in joy, seed that was sown in tears.

Brave heart! true soldier's son; set at thy post,
Deserting not till life itself was lost;

Thou faithful sentinel for others' weal,

Clad in a surer panoply than steel,

A resolute purpose,—sleep, as heroes sleep,—

Slain, but not conquered!   We thy loss must weep,

And while our sight the mist of sorrow dims,

Feel all these comforting words lie down like hymns

Hushed after service in cathedral walls;

But proudly on thy name thy country calls,

By thee raised higher than the highest place

Yet won by any of thy ancient race.

Be thy sons like thee!   Sadly as I bend

Above the page, I write thy name, lost friend!

With a friend's name this brief book did begin,

And a friend's name shall end it: names that win

Happy remembrance from the great and good;

Names that shall sink not in oblivion's flood,

But with clear music, like a church-bell's chime,

Sound through the river's sweep of onward rush-

    ing Time!

NOTES.

Note 1, page 101, line 13.

" Like her whose Shadow made the soldier's light.'

ERY sure I am that the great American poet, LONGFELLOW, would not refuse me permission to append here, in lieu of any note of explanation, his own beautiful lines on Miss Nightingale, alluding to the anecdote of a dying soldier pressing his lips to her shadow on the wall.

SANTA FILOMENA.

From the Atlantic Monthly.

Whene'er a noble deed is wrought,
Whene'er is spoken a noble thought,
  Our hearts, in glad surprise,
  To higher levels rise.

The tidal wave of deeper souls
Into our inmost being rolls,
 And lifts us unawares
 Out of all meaner cares.

Honor to those whose words or deeds
Thus help us in our daily needs,
 And by their overflow
 Raise us from what is low!

Thus thought I, as by night I read
Of the great army of the dead,
 The trenches cold and damp,
 The starved and frozen camp—

The wounded from the battle-plain,
In dreary hospitals of pain,
 The cheerless corridors,
 The cold and stony floors.

Lo! in that house of misery
A lady with a lamp I see
 Pass through the glimmering gloom,
 And flit from room to room.

And slow, as in a dream of bliss,
The speechless sufferer turns to kiss
 Her shadow, as it falls
 Upon the darkening walls.

As if a door in heaven should be
Opened, and then closed sud-lenly,
    The vision came and went,
    The light shown and was spent.

On England's annals, through the long
Hereafter of her speech and song,
    That light its rays shall cast
    From portals of the past.

A lady with a lamp shall stand
In the great history of the land,
    A noble type of good,
    Heroic womanhood.

Not even shall be wanting here
The palm, the lily, and the spear,
    The symbols that of yore
    Saint FILOMENA bore.

NOTE 2, page 104, 18th line.

"Sends to far nations noble Garaye's name."

I extract this note from the work of M. Odorici
which I mentioned in my Introduction.

"Parmi les découvertes heureuses et utiles que M. de
la Garaye fit dans ses expériences chimiques, nous citerons
particulièrement ce qu'il nommait *les sels essentiels*, tirés
des végétaux et des minéraux au moyen de l'eau mise en

mouvement sans l'aide du feu ni d'aucun autre agent
mécanique. Ces sels renfermant les principes les plus
actifs, fournirent des remèdes salutaires et jusqu'alors
musités.

"La nouvelle de cette découverte parvint aux oreilles
u Roi et excita la libéralité de S. M., dont le cœur com-
patissant ne se démentit jamais. Le Roi voulut que ces
secrets, trouvés et distribués pour ainsi dire dans le
silence, fussent rendus publics et que les bienfaits qui
devaient en résulter pussent se répandre dans toutes les
classes.

"Louis XV. le manda exprès à Marly en 1731, et,
après diverses expériences faites devant plusieurs person-
nages, le Roi, pour témoigner au comte de la Garaye sa
satisfaction toute particulière, lui fit compter 50,000 livres,
qui tournèrent au profit des pauvres et de la science.

"Plus tard le Roi lui envoya son portrait et celui de la
Reine, avec 25,000 livres pour une seconde découverte ;
plusieurs grands seigneurs, les princes du sang, et entre
autres le savant et trop calomnié duc d'Orléans, lui écri-
virent des lettres de félicitations, et l'imprimeur J.-B.
Coignard publia du comte de la Garaye, un mémoire in-
titulé : *Chimie hydraulique.*

"Aimé et honoré du Roi, il fut créé et 1725 chevalier
de l'Ordre royal et militaire de *Notre-Dame-du-Mont-
Carmel et de Saint-Lazare-de-Jérusalem.* En 1729, Mgr.
le duc d'Orléans l'éleva à la dignité de *Grand-Hospitalier*
(Commandeur) de ce même ordre pour la province de Bretagne.

"En 1746, le jeune duc de Penthièvre, accompagné du

marquis de Saint-Pern, étant venu pour présider les Etats de Bretagne, lui fit l'honneur de le visiter à la Garaye, d'y passer trois jours et de partager avec lui les occupations d'infirmier, objet de sa plus tendre sollicitude."

A curious phase of life, in a man who began his career as a gay young officer. He greatly distinguished himself at the siege of Namur, and was a brave and gallant soldier.

www.ingramcontent.com/pod-product-compliance
Lightning Source LLC
Chambersburg PA
CBHW022339020726
47500CB00004B/1188